CONTENTS

Nick looked at her from the point he was seated. "Are you free by 8pm?"

Isabella stood still. The question had hit her like a time bomb and she thought of the response to give. Despite knowing the man Nick was, she wanted to keep her distance.

Nick wasn't ready to give in to the silence that had spanned within some few seconds. "Dr. Chris invited me for a dinner, and I need a lady to go with me."

Isabella looked at her boss; she wasn't ready for games. "I will be free by then, but once it is 10pm I should be home."

Nick smiled. "I will come over to pick you up, and I will make sure you are home by 10pm."

CHAPTER 1

-Back Home-

Pastor Nick woke up from sleep with a burden in his heart. On two different nights within a week, he'd dreamt about a woman he lost contact with 22 years ago. He thought he'd forgotten about her, but now he knew better. Was God trying to speak to him, or was his past haunting him?

He recalled the last days he'd spent with the young lady; they were memories he wished he could get out of his mind. He'd lost his wife two years earlier and vowed never to have an affair with another lady. A transfer to Port Harcourt was on the card and he couldn't predict the future.

Upon resumption at Port Harcourt, he met this young lady. She was his secretary and before he could get his emotions to check, he'd found a soft spot for her and there was no going back.

Pastor Nick pulled himself from the bed. He needed to put the past behind him and go for his prayer walk. There was a beep on his phone and he reached for it.

Morning dad, the flight from Lagos to Abuja takes off by 2pm.

He'd forgotten that Edwin was returning to Abuja that Saturday, Edwin had arrived at Lagos late in the night on Friday. For three years, he was in California on a scholarship studying Business Finance;

now he was done. He wished Angela was alive to see their son grow, but she'd died after childbirth and he'd to leave Edwin with Aunt Sandra when he's transferred to Port Harcourt.

Aunt Sandra; such an amiable woman. She died of a heart attack. She didn't inform anyone of her health challenge, not even Pastor Nick, who was her favorite nephew.

Pastor Nick wondered if God loved him; taking away all the people he loved. He could only get one answer to the question each time it crept into his mind; God's way isn't ours. Nothing happens to a man without His knowledge and permission.

After putting the phone back in its place, Nick wrote a list of prayers on a note. He had made it a duty to pray for his family, friends, church members and the leaders of the country. That very day, he would make a special prayer for his secretary at Port Harcourt.

*****

Sally looked through the window, studying the environment. It was her first visit to Nigeria and her mother had

allowed her to take the trip together with

Edwin. She'd spent her entire life in

California with her mother and knew

nothing about her father. Each time she

asked, it made her mum mad at her.

She'd learned not to be pushy or incur

the wrath of a mother who had given her

the best life any child would wish for.

She'd met Edwin at a friend's birthday

party and the first contact they had sealed

a friendship that had become an intimate

relationship.

She was reluctant to attend the party that evening. At age nineteen, she was still shy and reserved. She wouldn't want to hurt her mother, but she had no choice. If she stayed back, Marian would've picked up a fight.

Alice, who was the event planner, had made a perfect choice of the dress she would put on; a red gown, and also insisted she left her hair loose and curled instead of her usual pony tail hair style.

When they'd arrived at the party venue, Sally found it difficult to blend with the others. Alice had her plans in place and hoped a young man would sweep her friend up from her boring lifestyle. Not too long, the three noble gentlemen; as they were called–Charlie, Peterson, and Edwin arrived. Charlie and Peterson were hooked, so they were out of the league. Unlike other young men, Edwin was not a player. He was by far a noble man than his friends. That wouldn't come as a surprise; he was a pastor's son.

While a live band performed on stage, most of the guests helped themselves to the dance floor. Among those who didn't bother to go over to the dance floor were Edwin and Sally.

Sally had a crush on Edwin, but she never mentioned it to anyone. She watched him from the point she's sitting, hoping to get his attention. Alice caught sight of her friend staring at Edwin. She walked up to her and whispered, "take your chance before someone else does."

Sally smiled and pulled away. She wasn't ready to get out of her shell and as every minute passed, she wished the party was over. Sally made haste to move to another section of the party hall to hide from

Alice; at that point, she missed a step. At

the brink of dropping to the floor like a

log of wood, she found herself in the safe

hands of a charming young man.

She felt the masculine touch and as she

opened her eyes, she felt a sudden heat

flow in her body.

"Thanks," she said, as she steadied

herself. She wondered how Edwin was

quick to save her from embarrassment.

Edwin smiled. "You are welcome."

He led her to a table, and they watched the others, who danced to the music that played. They had known each other at the University, but not on a personal level.

Edwin studied her for a while "Hope you're not hurt."

"I guess I'm fine." She pulled her shoes and examined her leg. "I'm perfectly okay."

They laughed over it and talked about several issues before Edwin took the bold step.

"Do you wish to dance?"

Sally felt the tension in her body. She wasn't good at dance, though she loved music. She could play the piano and the guitar like a pro. Sally wasn't sure if she should turn down the request.

"I take your silence as a no."

Edwin didn't feel bad, but Sally wouldn't want to ruin the good time they were having.

"I'm a terrible dancer," she said.

Edwin giggled. "I'm not a great dancer either, but I've been rehearsing."

Alice walked over to Sally. "Oh girl, I've been going around looking for you." Alice turned, her mouth opened wide at the sight of Edwin. She wasn't expecting to see him. "I hope I'm not intruding."

"No, you are not." Edwin stood up, willing to give the ladies a break. "I have to join my friends."

"Thanks for your time." Sally gave him a shy, girlish look.

Edwin felt that web of attraction and used the opportunity. "See you tomorrow."

"Thanks for staying around."

He gave a nod and left.

Alice looked at her friend, her ears spread out, waiting to hear the gist.

"Don't start." Sally knew her friend would heap loads of questions like a truck, and that was the last thing she wanted. In fact, she wouldn't want her friend to know Edwin had asked her for a dance. If she did, Alice would make a special announcement for the two to be brought to the dance floor.

"Alright, I seal my mouth." Alice pinned her mouth with her fingers, while Sally looked in the direction where Edwin had settled with his friends.

"Hey girl, you're tripping."

"No, I'm not." Sally gave that weary look. She wouldn't accept the obvious truth.

"I'm going to tell the others." Alice was up on her feet, ready to spill the good news.

"Please, don't. It won't make sense, and there is nothing going on between us."

Alice gave that nod of approval. "I see. You're protecting your man. Two Nigerians in love! What a coincidence."

*****

"That's the church." Edwin pointed at the building sited by the right.

Sally surveyed the building. "Wow! That must have cost a fortune."

"My dad would stop at nothing to see that money is available for any project that has God as the central figure." Edwin inhaled. "His passion for God's work surprises me. I wonder if I can ever have such a passion to do the work of God."

Sally placed her hands on Edwin's. "You do, but you've not realized it."

Jones took a right turn; within some few minutes, he parked in front of a duplex. He led a quick prayer of thanksgiving for the safe trip. The driver had learnt so much from Pastor Nick, who had made him understand it was necessary to thank

God after every trip and after every activity of the day.

"Welcome to my home."

Edwin held Sally's hands as she looked around the beautiful environment. The architectural design of the house was top-notch. She perceived she wouldn't have a dull moment. The environment was welcoming, and she hoped her meeting with Pastor Nick would be the same.

The door flung open and Gladys hurried to meet Edwin.

"Welcome home, sweetheart." She gave Edwin a warm embrace and a pinch on the cheek. She looked at Sally and back at Edwin. "O dear, you came home with a bride."

Edwin couldn't say a word; and watched as Gladys gave Sally a welcoming smile.

Gladys had been living with Pastor Nick ever since he got the call to start a ministry. She'd become like family and had seen Edwin grow to become the young man he was. Being an elderly woman with no one around, Pastor Nick had accommodated her in his house and despite employing her as a House Keeper; he never gave her chores to do.

"Your dad is in a meeting with the church council." Gladys led the way as they walked into the house. "He will be so delighted to see you."

She gave Sally and Edwin a warm smile before heading to the kitchen.

*****

Pastor Nick couldn't take his eyes off Sally. She looked familiar, but he couldn't tell where he'd met her. As they sat over

at dinner, he'd asked several questions

and none had given him a clue about

knowing her. Discovering how Sally and

his son had met; It reminded him of the

day he met Angela.

**

Nick had suffered an injury after a soccer

game with his friends and they had taken

him to the Specialist hospital. Jay's mum;

Nurse Glory worked at the hospital and

Nick hoped she would be the one to take

charge of his treatment. He knew she'd

be gentle on him; but when they arrived,
three operations were on and the
available nurses had to attend to other
issues. He had one choice; a student
nurse.

"No, I won't." Nick wouldn't allow a
student nurse to dress his wound, but not
too long, he changed his mind as Angela
walked into the ward. "What a damsel,"
he said.

He barely took his eyes off her and he
wished the treatment wasn't over when
she walked out of the ward.

After Angela had left the ward, he gave Jay a weird look. Being a person of like mind, Jay could tell what Nick had in mind.

"She's a student nurse, so don't be stupid."

Nick smiled. "I will take my shot. I won't let this gift pass me by."

Nick had gotten the best treatment he wished for and ensured he had a quality time discussing with Angela. From that day, he made it a point of duty to check on her. He wanted his relationship with

Angela to be a hit-and-run affair, but she changed him and each day that passed made him realize Angela was God sent. She was the only person who made him have a rethink about life and see reasons to serve God.

"Thank you, Jesus." Pastor Nick said, putting the past to rest.

"What is God saying?" Edwin had grown to know his father and anytime he uttered that phrase, "thank you, Jesus," there was a possibility that God must have dropped a revelation.

"I'm thinking about the good old days."
Pastor Nick took a deep breath and
closed his eyes.

"Sure, they were." Edwin always loved it
when his father told him stories of his past
events. It gave him that assurance of
God's master plan for everyone.

"I hope you like the food." Pastor Nick
starred at Sally. He wondered if she was
enjoying the pounded yam and Egusi
soup prepared by Gladys.

Sally nodded. "It's delicious and I see
reasons Edwin had insisted I try it."

Edwin smiled "I'm glad you love it. You owe me a gift for that."

Sally nodded. "A paid ticket to Prem Babeg's new movie would do."

Edwin looked at her. "Are you serious"

Gladys joined them at the table. "Anyone interested in coffee?"

"Of course I am." Pastor Nick wouldn't miss the opportunity of an evening coffee.

He gestured towards Sally, who gave a nod of approval.

"I'm in," she said.

Edwin looked at everyone. "I wouldn't want to be left out."

Gladys cut in. "Not under my watch. Even if no one is ready to serve you, I will."

"That's my mama." Edwin smiled as he held Gladys' hand.

CHAPTER 2

-Face to face with the past-

Isabella closed her eyes as she stood in front of the mirror. It was too late to withdraw the decision she'd made. She'd accepted the invitation to be at her cousin's 50th birthday party in Nigeria and had allowed Sally to leave a week earlier.

Thinking about Sally; she wouldn't give the young lady a chance to visit Nigeria, but this time she knew she was in safe hands. Edwin had proved several times that he differed from other young men, and that had made her accept her daughter's request to follow him to Nigeria.

What Isabella hadn't thought about was how she'd cope with a return to a country where memories would welcome her once she stepped foot on the soil.

She left the country when she found out she was pregnant after a wonderful time with her boss.

Would she ever forgive herself for running away without letting him know she's pregnant? What if their path crossed once again? Would he believe her story? How would she deal with this guilt that has turned into a burden? Would Sally ever forgive her for refusing to let her know the reason she'd left Nigeria?

"The cab is waiting, madam." Laura stood by the door, her eyes fixed on Isabella.

"Thanks." Isabella put the past behind and turned her attention to Laura, who was still standing at the entrance of the room.

Isabella owned a fashion house and had made a name in her line of business. Right from the moment she'd arrived in California, God had never abandoned her and was always there for her whenever she needed Him, but she had refused to give God a chance in her life.

She had that belief that she wasn't in God's plan despite the truth that stared at her right in the face.

*****

Edwin walked into the Church Office as soon as his father raised his head after making that silent prayer.

Pastor Nick had a timetable and plan for his daily routine and Edwin knew where to find him at that very hour of the day, unless there was an emergency.

Pastor Nick had made it known to his close allies he was a man of all; and he would reschedule his daily routine if people needed his attention. That was his first duty as a priest, *a call to serve*; and he had vowed never to neglect that duty.

"What's up, son? Going somewhere?"

"Sally's mum is arriving today, so I'll be going over to the airport to pick her."

"Is there something you're not telling me?" Pastor Nick walked up to his son. "Wait, don't tell me I'm out of the picture of your wedding plan."

Edwin looked at his dad, amazed. He didn't mention getting married to Sally, but he had that in mind.

"Son, I know you better than you think. Though we haven't had time to talk, but seeing you with that young lady for a week now is enough to let me know what's going on." He gave Edwin a pat on the back. "I haven't spent a lot of time with her, but I approve of the relationship you two are having, and remember to keep the marriage bed holy."

Edwin stood still. His dad had gotten a better side of him. Sally was a lady he respected. Well trained, well behaved and God fearing, despite her background. He wondered how Sally didn't end up being a spoilt kid; maybe that's a credit to Isabella. She was a disciplinarian and wouldn't let Sally grow up to be influenced by negative vices. The only thing that disconnected Sally and her mum was the fact that Sally showed interest in church activities, but Isabella-no way, she still had her reservations.

"If she's God's will for my life, I won't let her go." Edwin wouldn't give in to his father's conclusive statement for now.

"Drive safe and tell them I will be around later in the evening."

"Sure, I will."

Immediately Edwin stepped out, Pastor Nick walked back to his seat. "Thank you, Lord."

He was always thankful to God because Edwin didn't grow up the way he did. He'd been a club guy back in the days.

Hanged out with friends, went about

drinking, chasing women and attempted

smoking, but didn't find pleasure in it.

It was God's grace that helped him give

up his wayward life and the woman he'd

cherished most was responsible.

The thought of Angela made him wish she

was still with him, but she had fulfilled her

time on earth.

**

The pain of the labor Angela had endured

relived itself. Nick had been at work that

afternoon. Something hadn't been right throughout that day; from the meeting with the company's executives and the argument he'd had with Jay. He wondered why he wasn't thinking straight and as he sat at his desk ready to have a rest; his phone rang. It was Angela; he picked up, but she didn't say a word. Nick picked up his car keys and left the office.

He'd maneuvered his way through the busy traffic and thank goodness he hadn't been involved in a crash. God had led him home safe that very day. He'd thought it was his ability, but when he'd

given his life over to the work of God, he

knew it was God's plan to keep him.

Getting home, there laid Angela groaning

in pain. He couldn't tell how long she'd

been lying there helpless and he couldn't

think straight. Different thoughts were

running through his mind. Every second

counted, and he helped her into the car

and headed for the hospital.

While at the hospital, they had rushed her

to the labor room while he paced around.

An hour later, Nurse Glory had come out

to see him. From her expression, he could read the mixed feeling.

He went into the ward where Angela was and there she laid - lifeless, while the innocent baby was sleeping in the court. He couldn't hold himself as he wept. Not minding what had transpired earlier that the day, Jay had come over to meet him.

For days, he couldn't sleep; he'd lost *a priceless jewel*. The thought of the plans they'd penned down for the baby made things worse.

The company knew what was best, and they transferred him to Benin City; where Aunt Sandra lived. There, he found solace, and vowed never to let any other woman into his life again until he received another transfer to Port Harcourt.

*****

Isabella stepped out of the bathroom after a cold shower. She needed to freshen up and take a nap after the journey. She was a strong woman and now in her forties; Isabella knew she needed to take things easy and spend time to relax. At that age, she'd noticed the strands of grey hair. That reminded her; she'd missed her appointment with Douglas. She's meant to meet him for a retouch, but she'd have to wait for another two weeks when she returned to U. S together with Sally.

Will Sally be willing to leave at once? She didn't think about that all the while. She wouldn't pressure the young lady to go with her. Sally had marked her 21st birthday three months earlier and, as a full-grown adult, she had the right to decide her future. Having fallen in love with Edwin and Abuja city; as well as her

positive remarks about Pastor Nick; the

signs were obvious she wouldn't leave

immediately.

Talking about Pastor Nick, the name

reminded her of her boss at Port

Harcourt, but she doubted if her boss

would ever become a priest.

Isabella believed it would be a great

honor to meet with a priest who is the

namesake of the man she'd loved in her

youth. She'd heard so many good things

about him and his relationship with

people. Maybe he would be the man God
would send to solve the puzzle
surrounding her life.

*****

Pastor Nick couldn't hide his excitement
as he anticipated his meeting with Sally's
mother. Edwin had said positive things
about the woman and he was eager to
meet her; more so that he'd come to
terms with her daughter.

Both men came out of the car as Edwin
parked. Edwin led the way as they

walked to the building that was just some few steps away.

Before they got to the doorpost, Sally met them. She'd sighted them afar off and had saved them from the stress of using the doorbell.

Edwin and Sally were the first to go in before Pastor Nick entered. A step further and Pastor Nick got the shock of his life.

For a moment, he froze. "Isabella!" It was an unimaginable moment, and Pastor Nick had his eyes fixed on her.

"Nick!" This must be a dream, Isabella thought, but it wasn't as the man she'd once loved stood before her.

Sally and Edwin were speechless as they watched their parents, who stood at a spot staring at each other. Pastor Nick took a bold step and attempted to move close to Isabella; she withdrew herself and backed out.

"Mom!" Sally ran after Isabella, leaving the guests.

"What's going on?" Edwin looked at his

dad, demanding answers to the act he

and Isabella had just put up.

CHAPTER 3

-The unforgettable memories-

Pastor Nick sat in the church office. He couldn't think straight. Sally looked familiar, but he never thought she's Isabella's daughter. Now that he'd seen them together, the resemblance was visible. The dream he'd weeks back had become clearer. God had made him dream of Isabella to prepare him for this moment. Where would he start his story?

He looked at Edwin, who had been standing all the while. The young man needed answers to the situation at hand. Silently, he prayed. "God, you are always faithful. Help me."

Pastor Nick pointed to a chair. "Please, sit."

Reluctantly, Edwin dragged himself to a seat as he waited patiently to listen to the story that had transpired in his childhood.

*****

"Good morning, sir." The voice of a young lady welcomed Nick as soon as he walked down the hallway leading to his office. The lady made haste to get his briefcase and led the way into the office, while Nick followed.

Getting in, he looked around; the office was in an excellent condition. All the equipment and files he would need were in place and arranged just the way he'd instructed. He helped himself to a seat; at that moment, he noticed the young lady was still standing waiting for further instructions.

"Is there anything I can do for you, sir?"

Nick smiled. He'd been told the young lady was on her first job and it meant he would need to tutor her and help her become good at her job. From the impression she'd given him, she wasn't doing badly. "How long have you been working here?"

"I joined the organization three months ago."

"Grab a seat."

Nick could be a tough man, but as much as he was the boss, he hated to see those working under him feel uncomfortable, and as he looked straight in the eyes of the young lady, she's innocent, naïve and needed to grow up. "How old are you?"

"Twenty." Her response was quick and her voice shaky. The tension growing in her was clear. She'd heard about Nick and was told he didn't tolerate ill mannered behavior and lazy workers. She hoped she wouldn't fall into his black book, so she would do all in her power to impress him.

"Sorry, I didn't ask of your name."

"Isabella Matthews," she replied.

The panic was more this time; Nick read it in her expression and he needed to help her kill that spirit.

"I would like to know more about you in a minute or two." He brought out a pen and a notepad. Nick hadn't planned their first meeting to be an interview session, but all he wanted was to build Isabella's confidence.

Isabella looked at him straight in the eyes. She'd practiced what he'd asked her to do several times before she got the job. She knew how well to introduce herself, although Nick had caught her unawares.

Minutes later, she was up on her feet. She'd done an excellent introduction and Nick had seen the confidence in her.

Weeks had passed, and Isabella had coped with Nick's excesses. She knew what he wanted, how he wanted it, and she'd planned his daily routine just the way he'd taught her. She'd learnt so much from the man, and she's more of a professional now than the time she'd started.

Nick sat at his table, wondering who to take along with him for a dinner party, which a client had invited him to attend. He couldn't say no. Angela had made him a changed man, and he'd stopped

messing around with women. Back in the

days, he'd call on any of his girlfriends to

accompany him for the dinner, but at that

moment, it was a different ball game.

Isabella walked into the office after a

busy day. "I will take my leave, sir."

Nick looked at her from the point he was

seated. "Are you free by 8pm?"

Isabella stood still. The question had hit

her like a time bomb and she thought of

the response to give. Despite knowing

the man Nick was, she wanted to keep
her distance.

Nick wasn't ready to give in to the silence
that had spanned within some few
seconds. "Dr. Chris invited me for a
dinner, and I need a lady to go with me."

Isabella looked at her boss; she wasn't
ready for games. "I will be free by then,
but once it is 10pm I should be home."

Nick smiled. "I will come over to pick you
up, and I will make sure you are home by
10pm."

She turned her back to leave while Nick

breathed a fresh air of relief.

**

A knock on the door and Nick was

amazed. He wondered if the lady

standing before him was the same person

who served as his secretary at work. She

was an epitome of beauty and everything

about her reflected beauty. He had to put

his emotions to check, so he positioned

his mind on the fact that he needed her

for just that evening.

"Thanks for accepting the offer." He led her to the car and at every given opportunity he stole a gaze.

Isabella knew the effect she had on men and she'd never doubted the possibility of pulling men down if she wanted to be a seductress. Thank God she was an ambitious woman with a career in focus.

**

Arriving at the party venue, Nick had introduced Isabella to several people as a friend and not his secretary at work. He'd told her to place herself high, and she'd performed excellently. Now seated at a

corner of the building, she couldn't

imagine that a man as hard as a rock

while on official duty would be so calm.

She found it hard to place Nick on the list

of men she'd encountered. He was totally

different and had that personality that

attracted people. He was a man of

charisma. Though she'd heard about

some of his past; his late wife, and how he

needed to start life all over; that evening

she promised to help him go beyond a

dinner date as long as the relationship

was *Platonic*.

**

Months passed by at the speed of light and the relationship between the two became stronger. Nick had tried to resist the urge to go intimate with Isabella, but his emotions had gotten a better part. He'd taken her out frequently; they'd had a good time at the beach, attended dinner parties and watched movies at the theatre. She was a lovely young lady to be with, and every moment with her was entertaining. Gradually, Nick realized the thought of Angela was fading.

**

Things took a turn on that chilly Friday morning. Nick had hoped to receive the charming and welcoming smile as he entered the office, but Isabella wasn't there. He picked his phone to place a call; the number was unreachable. Has something happened to Isabella? He summoned courage and pulled himself together. He would wait for some minutes. If she didn't call or show up, he would check on her.

An hour was gone, then two hours; still there's no sight of her, neither was there a message from her. He wasn't comfortable any longer, so he left the office.

**

When he arrived at Isabella's house, he knocked on the door. There was no response. After several trials, he decided it was time to leave. At that point, Musa; a next-door neighbor met him.

"I *dey* find Isabella?"

"Yes." Nick felt a sudden relief. "Did she tell you where she was going?"

Musa nodded in response and brought out an envelope. *"She say make I give you."*

He gave the envelope to Nick and walked back to his house. Nick looked at the envelope, wondering why Isabella had written him a letter. He imagined what the content of the letter would be. Was it a resignation letter or something else?

He found a chair by the corner; sat down and opened the envelope. The note written was just a few lines. At least it

wasn't a resignation letter. That gave Nick

some hope, but alas, it was worse than

the content of a resignation letter.

*Thanks for the time we shared. It will
always be in my memory.*

With love,

Bella.

Nick was torn apart, and his world was at

a halt. Another woman had just gone out

of his life, or could it be one of her pranks

He settled for the latter thought, but after

days, weeks and months passed, he knew

it was over. That was the limit; never again would his heart be open to any woman. He wished he'd rejected the transfer to Port Harcourt. At least he would have remained loyal to his vows; now he'd have to retake them all over.

*****

Pastor Nick stood up from his seat and looked out through the window. "For twenty-two years, I didn't hear from Isabella, until today." He walked back to the desk and watched his son, who sat quietly. "I don't even know the reason she'd left."

Edwin looked at his father. This time, he pitied the man standing before him. "You still have time to ask her."

*****

"Is he my father?" Sally couldn't hide her feelings. She's boiling in anger and needed clarifications. If her mother had explained things to her at the right time, it wouldn't have gotten to this point.

Isabella raised her head. "No, he isn't."

She could see the rage in her daughter's

eyes.

Now she'd open up. The secret she'd

kept for the past years had imprisoned

her, and she needed to be free from the

burden.

"Come over." She beckoned on Sally to

join her.

The young lady dragged her feet towards

her mother. As much as it hurt to be put in

the dark, she loved her mum so much she

would do whatever she wanted.

*****

September 23rd, year 2000, was a day

Isabella would never forget. Nick had

promised to pick her up by 7pm for a

dinner. She'd waited for him, but he

didn't show up. She'd called his phone; it

was off. The executives were having a

meeting that afternoon before she'd left

the office, but none of their meetings

lasted for over five hours. If on that very

day it did, Nick would call or send a

message. She knew tempers rose and

emotions got hurt whenever there was an

executive meeting and most of the

managers would come out wearing a strong face. If such had happened, she still believed Nick would call.

It might be one of his tests to know her reactions. She wouldn't fail that test. She'd passed every test Nick had come up with and that very day, she would pass another; so she'd thought.

Out of curiosity, she left her house.

**

Standing at the doorpost, she knocked on the door. Thankfully, she heard footsteps

approaching. The door opened; it wasn't
Nick, but Jay who stood at the entrance.

"Come on in." Jay spoke in a calm tune as
he allowed Isabella into the house.

She didn't hesitate. Jay was Nick's friend;
he'd been around for a visit and she
thought she could trust him. He brought
her a glass of water; innocently, she
accepted it.

"Where is Nick?"

"He stepped out." Jay was a good liar, and it wasn't hard to come up with one. "I think he's supposed to meet you."

Isabella nodded, "Yes."

It was true Nick was to come over, but Jay knew the game he's playing at that point. "Do you care for a cup of coffee? At least you should have something to drink before Nick returns." Jay knew how to sweep a lady off her feet and, at that moment, he knew Isabella wouldn't have a choice. He was her boss' friend, so she would know better than reject his offer.

"I wouldn't mind." She faked a smile, hoping he would leave and allow her to have sometime to herself until Nick returned.

Few minutes had passed, still Nick wasn't back. She'd called his phone again, still switched off. Jay met her holding two cups of coffee. He handed one over to her while he sat down and helped himself with the second.

"Why is he out for so long?" Isabella felt uncomfortable as she took a sip of the coffee.

The coffee wasn't too hot, so she would take a gulp and leave if Nick didn't return within the next five minutes.

Jay came up with another perfect lie. "Probably he is discussing business. You know how it goes in this line of work."

"Hmm, yeah, I do." Isabella sensed the danger of staying longer. She'd just realized Nick's car outside. Isabella took three gulps of the coffee and emptied the cup. "I have to go now," she said.

Isabella stood up, picked her bag and tried to take a step, but her legs were numb. What was going on? Suddenly she felt dizzy and before she could get hold of herself, she went blank.

**

The next time Isabella opened her eyes, she found herself in bed. How did she get in there? She turned, trying to think of how she'd got herself into the room.

She was naked; and just by the side of the bed, Jay was seated, adjusting his shirt.

"What did you do to me?"

"Relax girl. You are so sweet." He got up and wiped his face with a towel. "So bad you are still a virgin, but I will be gentle on you."

Isabella rose in anger, got dressed, and walked straight to the door. She slid the handle of the door; it was locked. She looked at Jay.

"I'm sorry dear." Jay walked slowly towards her. "It's just the two of us in here, and we are going to have a good time."

Isabella was gripped with fear. "Where is Nick?" She felt insecure, and every second spelt doom.

"Nick isn't returning today. He actually left a note behind to inform you he had an emergency meeting at Lagos."

Jay cornered the young lady, and there was no way to escape as she leaned on the door. She could feel the masculine sensation that emitted from Jay's body, but she wouldn't give in to his antics. Her heart was pounding.

"Please, let me go and I won't say a word about what has happened to Nick."

Jay smiled and caressed her hair. "I know you've always wanted Nick to have sex with you." He placed a kiss on her forehead. She closed her eyes, trembling in fear. "He wouldn't do that. He is yet to get over Angela and he is only using you to forget his past."

"Please, stop it. Let me go." She was aggressive and ready to fight her way to freedom.

Jay pulled away; for a moment, Isabella felt relieved.

"Open the door so I can leave; please."

"It's late in the night and I can't let go of you." Jay watched her and slowly he unbuttoned his shirt. "You've come to a lion's den and there is no escape route."

Isabella trembled in fear. Now it was over. She wouldn't have anywhere to hide. No one would come to her rescue. Even if she screamed at the top of her voice, no one would hear her. Tears rolled down her eyes, but Jay cared less.

He wanted her and he would have her.

*****

Isabella looked at her daughter. "A
month after that incidence, I found out I
was pregnant. The last thing on my mind
was an abortion and if I stayed longer in
Port Harcourt, Nick would know, so I left."

The thought of how good Nick had been
to her made the pain worse. At that point,
Isabella couldn't hide the tears as they
poured out like running water.

"I left him a note expressing how thankful I was for the time we shared and I told him the truth about the love I had for him." Isabella brought out her handkerchief and wiped her tears. "I contacted my neighbor who told me he gave the letter to Nick, and that was the last time I attempted to know how he was faring."

Sally tried to restrain herself from crying, but she couldn't. She fought the tears that had formed in her eyes. "So, my father was a rapist."

Those words hit Isabella deep in the heart. The manner with which she'd Sally's pregnancy made her grief, but each time she'd thought of it, she pushed the thoughts aside. "No, you were God's gift to me." She wiped her tears once more. "Of a truth, I hate the man who got me pregnant, but I always loved you as though you were Nick's child."

Sally threw her arms around her mum and gave her a warm embrace before firing another shot. "Tell Pastor Nick all that happened."

Isabella stood up and looked away. What her daughter wanted her to do was a hard task. How would she face Pastor Nick after all these years? The pain, the hurt he will feel. It wouldn't be easy. He might even hate her forever. "I can't. I don't know what to tell him."

Sally walked up to her mother. She held her hands. "You can write it, just the way you wrote to him when you left." Sally placed her hand on her mother's shoulder. "If you don't have the courage to give him the letter, I will do it for you."

"How do I write it? Oh God, I don't know what to do anymore."

"We are in this together, mum. Just pen down the first line and everything you want him to know would follow." Sally gave her that assuring smile.

Isabella saw her past relive itself. What she'd found difficult to do twenty-two years ago, she would do it now. If she starts the letter, would she have the courage to end it? So much was running through her mind.

CHAPTER 4

- The work of grace -

Edwin walked up to Sally, who had called

to inform him she was outside the

building. He wondered what Isabella

must have told Sally and the condition she

would be at that moment. He prayed the

women won't be hurt in the heart.

"Hi." Edwin gave Sally a warm embrace.

"How is your mum?" Edwin knew Isabella would be the one on the receiving end of all that had transpired.

"She's still trying to get over the past, and that's why I came over."

Edwin held Sally's hands. It's cold. "Are you okay?"

Sally nodded. "I don't think so. I feel sick."

"Let's go inside; Mama Gladys will get you something to warm you up."

She looked away. The thought of how her mother conceived her made her sick. She wished a day like this never came. "Don't bother. My condition is beyond any medical attention."

That statement was frightening. Edwin looked into her eyes. "What did your mum tell you?"

Sally inhaled deeply. "We will talk about it later, but I have to speak with your dad first."

"Now!" Edwin was troubled. If Sally wanted to speak with his dad, it meant there was more to the issue than what he'd heard.

"Yes, now." Sally was more resolute.

"He should be in the church office. We were together about an hour ago and he is yet to come home."

Sally knew the time was drawing near when emotions would be hurt. That realization made her tremble. Her eyes flickered with tears. Edwin was worried. The lady he'd fallen in love with was not herself and he'd never seen her this way before; confused and frail.

Sally didn't want the tears to pour out while standing with Edwin. He would end up babysitting her. She needed to leave at once.

"I will come over to the house to see you when I'm done." Her voice was shaky.

Edwin let go of her hands and looked into her eyes. "If you want me to come with you, I will."

Sally nodded and turned her back on him. He wouldn't go after her. She needed that time alone, and he believed after meeting his dad, Sally would feel much better. He watched her until she was out of sight.

*****

Pastor Nick sat down, thinking of the message to pen down for service the next day. He'd come up with two different topics which he believed the members of his church would love, but at some point, God had clearly shown him not to go ahead. He'd torn four sheets from his notepad and as he sat, he looked blank. This was not the first time such a thing had happened. He'd experienced it several times in his fifteen years of

ministerial work, and each time it

occurred, he knew God had a special

plan.

"Good evening, sir."

Pastor Nick looked towards the door. It's

sally. He wasn't expecting her. "Come in,

dear."

His secretary was told to give Sally a free

entrance whenever she came around.

Pastor Nick loved her like a father and

after the incidence that had occurred

earlier; he knew with time; the bond would get stronger.

Sally walked in and sank into the visitor's chair. There was always that peace she felt within her whenever she's with Pastor Nick. Knowing him for just a week seemed as if she'd known him for so long.

"How is Isabella?" Sally noticed Pastor Nick's expression. He'd that concerned look.

"Still trying to pick up the pieces of her past." Sally was blunt. The entire scenario had devastated her mum.

Pastor Nick nodded. "And you; how are you coping?"

"I still think I'm dreaming."

"It will be alright, my dear." Pastor Nick gave her a reassuring look. "God has a reason for everything."

"I hope so." She wondered how the man of God would feel when he finally reads the letter her mum had written to him. *What would be his reaction? Will he still trust God? Will he forgive his friend for his abominable act?*

Everything seemed out of place. *Will Pastor Nick be able to repeat the statement he'd uttered?*

As the thoughts flooded in Sally's mind, she thought there was no point in giving the letter to Pastor Nick. It would take great faith and grace of God for him to be stable for the morning service the next day. The content of the letter would be more devastating than the last her mum had written to him when she'd left.

"Is something bothering you?" Pastor Nick, in his wealth of experience as a priest and as a leader in an organization, sensed the emotional battle sally was struggling with.

Sally stood up and brought out a letter from her bag. "My mum asked me to give you." She handed the enveloped letter to Pastor Nick.

"Thanks." He smiled as he received the letter.

Sally knew the smile would fade away when he read the letter. She stood up and with a sad look in her eyes; she walked out of the office.

Pastor Nick opened the letter and made a silent prayer "God give me grace." As he read each line, he imagined the entire scenario. Unable to help it, he allowed the tears to roll down. Isabella had written a complete narrative of all that had happened that night. She made sure she didn't leave out any detail. Pastor Nick couldn't believe it. Though he was a man of God, but that moment he grieved. His friend had backstabbed him.

Jay had died some few months earlier and on his dying bed he'd asked Pastor Nick to forgive him. Pastor Nick had told him he held nothing against him, but right now, it had become clearer.

"Thank you Jesus." Pastor Nick folded the letter and put it back in the envelope. He wiped his eyes and suddenly he heard a hymn playing in the church. It was one of his favorite hymns; the old rugged cross.

*****

Sally played the chords passionately as she allowed the tears to flow. She needed a hymn that would take away her pains and worries, and God had given her the hymn for the moment. Despite the condition that had beset her entire family, she was ready to cling to the old, rugged cross. Jesus had paid the price for all her burden and all she's going through at that moment were trials of faith. Getting to the last verse of the hymn, she stopped. She couldn't keep up.

"That was angelic." Pastor Nick's voice was calm.

"Did you read the letter?" Sally believed if Pastor Nick had read that letter, he wouldn't be as calm as he was.

Gently, Pastor Nick walked up to her where she's seated. "I did. I read every word."

Sally was amazed. "What kind of man are you?" As much as she tried to understand that he was a man of God, she just didn't want to accept the fact that anyone who's betrayed in such a manner could stand firm.

Pastor Nick smiled and placed his arms on her shoulder. "I'm a man who's been broken." He gave a soft laugh. "I have been through the dark walls of this world.

I have lived a reckless life in the past and had faced turbulent situations where it seemed all hope was lost." He was silent for a while. "Despite all that had happened, God kept me. Just like the hymn you played, ever since I clung to the old rugged cross, God has been there for me and He took the burdens off me."

Sally looked at Pastor Nick. Never had she seen a man with so much trust and confidence in God. She couldn't hide her feelings anymore, and she wept bitterly. Pastor Nick comforted her, assuring her that all would be alright.

After she'd stopped grieving, she stood up, ready to lay the final burden that was on her mind.

"Where can I meet my father?"

The question didn't come as a surprise. Pastor Nick knew she would want to know where her father was. He'd counseled people who'd faced similar situations and have been in the crossroad of life. Unfortunately for Sally, she would never meet her father on earth. He held her hands and the memories of the last time he'd been with Jay came to mind.

*****

Jay laid in the bed feeling sorry. He knew his time on earth was ending. He recounted how he'd wasted his life. Jay looked at Pastor Nick. "Oh! What a useless life I've lived. All along, I had things going my way, but I slowly dragged myself into the arms of the devil. Why didn't I listen to you all the time you spoke to me about Christ? Why didn't I yield to your warning to let go of my evil ways? Look at me, what else can I do with my life?"

"Bro, stop complaining and give thanks to God for giving you a second chance. It is better that you've realized your mistake and accepted Christ than dying in sin."

That word hit Jay. Of a truth he'd finally given himself up to God, but there was a burden in his heart. He didn't know how to let go of the burden.

"Nick!" Jay held the hands of his friend.

"I'm still here with you."

"I have done great evil against you." Jay struggled to speak. "Please forgive me."

It grieved Pastor Nick. He knew his friend was really sorry for whatever wrong he'd done. "I hold nothing against you. From the depth of my heart, I forgive you."

"Thank you, my good friend." He took in a deep breath. "Please, pray for me one more time so I can rest in the bosom of Abraham."

Tears of joy and pain formed in Nick's eyes as he closed his eyes to pray for his friend. "Father in heaven, if it's your will to take Jeremiah home, please forgive him of all his iniquities and accept him in your kingdom. Amen."

Jay smiled. "I will see you in heaven someday. God bless your ministry."

Jay closed his eyes and gave up. Pastor Nick bent his head.

*****

"Your father is up there in heaven smiling; knowing you are in fine."

Sally stared at Pastor Nick. His reaction to issues baffled him. "If my father had actually told you what he did, would you have forgiven him?"

That was a complicated question. Sally was just as smart as her mother. Pastor Nick had noticed that in the way she expressed herself.

"Twenty-two years ago, probably I wouldn't have the grace to forgive him, but now, definitely, I would have forgiven him."

Sally felt some relief after seeing Pastor Nick's reaction to the entire situation. Of course, he was human and expressed his grief and pain; he still allowed the Holy

Spirit play a role in helping him. She

needed such grace in her life.

CHAPTER 5

- Nailing it to the cross -

Christ Field Ministry had a maximum capacity crowd as people trooped in to attend the Saturday morning service. It was a program that Pastor Nick had set aside for every first Saturday of every quarter and it had imparted people's life.

The last 24 hours had several mixed feelings for the Pastor. He'd met Isabella after twenty-two years; he'd discovered his best friend had committed an abominable act, and he's yet to receive a message from God on what to preach.

The choir members were in high spirit as they led the congregation in praise before rounding the session up with an atmosphere of worship. As they marched back to their seats, the congregation applauded. It was time for the message.

Pastor Nick walked to the altar. As his usual habit, he made a quiet prayer to God. "Father, help me."

The members knew the first word Pastor Nick would utter; *God bless the choir*, but on this day, it was different.

"Brethren, thank God for this wonderful day."

Some members looked one to another, still waiting to hear the usual comment.

"Today, I have the honor of inviting a guest to the podium and she would minister alongside me."

That was strange, and some members whispered among themselves. Was the man standing before them, Pastor Nick, or someone else?

"Sally Matthews, please, can I have you here with me at the podium?"

Sally was surprised as Pastor Nick called her upstage. She looked at Edwin, who sat next to her. He wondered what Pastor Nick had in mind. Sally wasn't a priest and didn't perform any special

ministerial duty back in California.

"Just do whatever he says," said Edwin.

Sally took a bold step and walked

towards Pastor Nick. Some congregants

whistled while others applauded as she

mounted the podium to meet Pastor Nick.

He held Sally's hand. "This beautiful lady

is the daughter of a close friend of mine,

and today I believe God would bless

each one through our joint ministration."

Edwin was praying deep in his heart. He knew his father was an anointed man of God, but Sally wasn't a lady who would face a crowd. "God, please help her."

Pastor Nick whispered to Sally, and she walked to the piano stand.

Pastor Nick said the word of prayer. "God Almighty, take charge and speak to us in Jesus' name."

"Amen," the congregation echoed in unison.

Sally ran some scales before she started

playing the tune of the old rugged cross.

As the hymn played, Pastor Nick

preached.

"Brethren!" He looked from one direction

to another. "There comes a time in the life

of a man when he would have to report

his deeds to his maker."

There was silence within the building.

People were eager to receive powerful

declarations from the throne of grace.

"There comes a time when all you have

done while on earth would stare at you

right in the face while standing at the

throne of judgment."

Pastor Nick was quiet for a moment and

as the hymn played, the words felt more

touching.

"There comes a time when those secrets

which you have buried with you are

revealed, and the past walks right beside

you and defines your present and your

future."

Some members couldn't bear the heat

and guilt that the message had hit them

with and they rolled on the floor, making

atonement for their deeds.

"Brethren, what is that past event, sin and

act that has formed a web around your

life? What is that deed that is serving as a

hindrance to your walk with God?"

Pastor Nick was quiet and at that moment,

Sally played another hymn–*it pays to

serve Jesus*. Pastor Nick knew the spirit of

God had led her. "Thank you, Jesus," he

said. The words of the hymn were

touching, people were weeping; lives

were receiving a new touch. Many had

come for prophetic declarations, but the service had turned out to be a rededication of souls.

"Are you still a soldier of Christ? Are you still standing at that post where God had placed you? Have you deviated from the plan which God has for you?"

Pastor Nick tried to round up, but the spirit didn't permit him. He went further to speak. "What is that burden that you are still bearing? It is time to lay it at the feet of Jesus. What is that worry, trouble and pain that has disconnected you from

God? Nail it to the cross of Calvary. God is ready to give you another chance."

At the end of the message, Pastor Nick beckoned to the members to sing the hymn all over.

At the close of the service that morning, most of the members walked quietly out of the church. The Holy Spirit had worked on them and, unlike their usual practice, they didn't stay back to chat.

Pastor Nick looked around. He was thankful to God for a glorious service. Earlier, he'd thought God didn't want him to preach, but knowing God's way isn't the same as that of man, he'd allowed God to take charge of the entire service.

"Pastor Nick!"

Pastor Nick looked back; turning his attention to the voice that had called on him. It was Isabella. She's shivering and from the look on her face, he could tell she'd cried her heart out.

She forced words from her mouth. "Do you think God can accept me after all these years?"

The words pierced through Pastor Nick's heart. Isabella had been broken, and he needed to help her amend the pieces of her wounded heart. He held her hands and looked into her eyes.

"If God can be merciful to me and use me as a tool in his vineyard, then he will also accept you."

Tears filled Isabella's eyes. She wanted God to help her, but her problem was how to go about it.

"Isabella, how long do you want to keep on having a walk with the past? It is time to move on. Give God a chance in your life and he will amend your broken heart."

Isabella knelt down. It was now or never. "Oh! God, please help me. Save me from this ocean. I am drowning, Lord. Please come to my rescue."

Pastor Nick watched as she poured her heart to God. He was glad that she'd summoned the courage to allow God to take hold of her. When she was done, she was up on her feet,

"I'm sorry, Nick." She was being honest. She wanted to get rid of the past.

Nick smiled. He was happy she'd done the most important thing; giving God charge over her life. "You will always remain dear to me, no matter what." He placed her head on his chest and looked up. "Thank you, Lord, for this day."

THE END

At times, we are faced with challenges, troubles and issues that seem unbearable. Through all these trials, we must always remember that God is with us and would never forsake us. Trust in Him and He would surely come to your aid when you need Him the most.

For questions and comments:

Contact email: premsoko1@gmail.com